THIS WALKER BOOK BELONGS TO:

For Banana Ted, from Banana Mummy x

First published 2020 by Walker Books Ltd, 87 Vauxhall Walk, London SE11 5HJ

This edition published 2021

10 9 8 7 6 5 4 3 2 1

© 2020 Yasmeen Ismail

This book has been typeset in Walbaum

Printed in China

British Library Cataloguing in Publication Data: a catalogue record for this book is available from the British Library

ISBN 978-1-4063-9422-1

www.walker.co.uk

Would You Like a
BANANA?

Yasmeen Ismail

WALKER BOOKS
AND SUBSIDIARIES
LONDON • BOSTON • SYDNEY • AUCKLAND

I'm hungry.

Would you like a banana?

No. It's too yellow. It's too bendy.

It is too wonky.

I won't eat a banana.

But you might *like* a banana.

Just try a teeny taste.

Would you like one on a plate?

No.

No.

You might like one with some bread,
or maybe standing on your head.

I won't eat a banana.

What about a little one?

Or maybe one that's in a bun?

No. I won't

How about I eat one too,
is that something *we* can do?

No. I won't
BAN

You might like it in the end.

In a bowl?

With a friend?

No. I won't eat a banana.

Watch its yellow belly
wobble on a happy jelly.

Upside-down or right way up,
mash it in your favourite cup.

Bananas can be
good with honey.

Slice it up,
pretend it's money.

Pop a candle on
and make
a very special
birthday cake.

There are so
many ways how.
Would you like to
eat one now?

No. I won't eat a BANANA!
That's what I SAID!

I won't eat one with some bread,

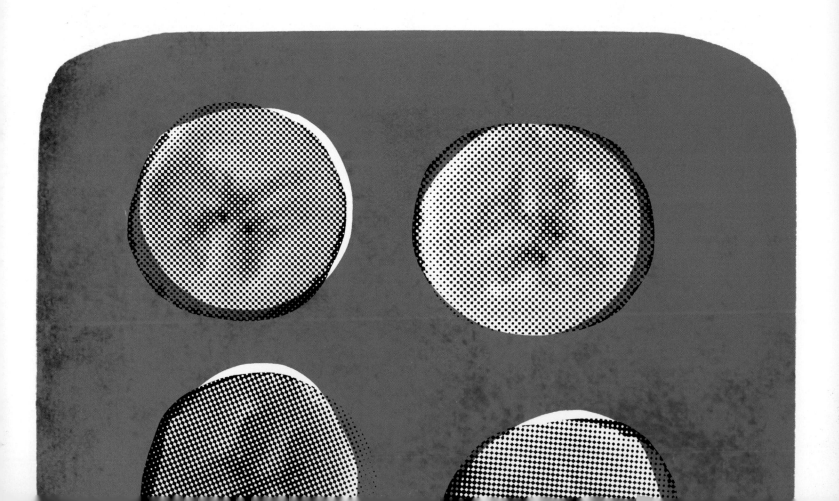

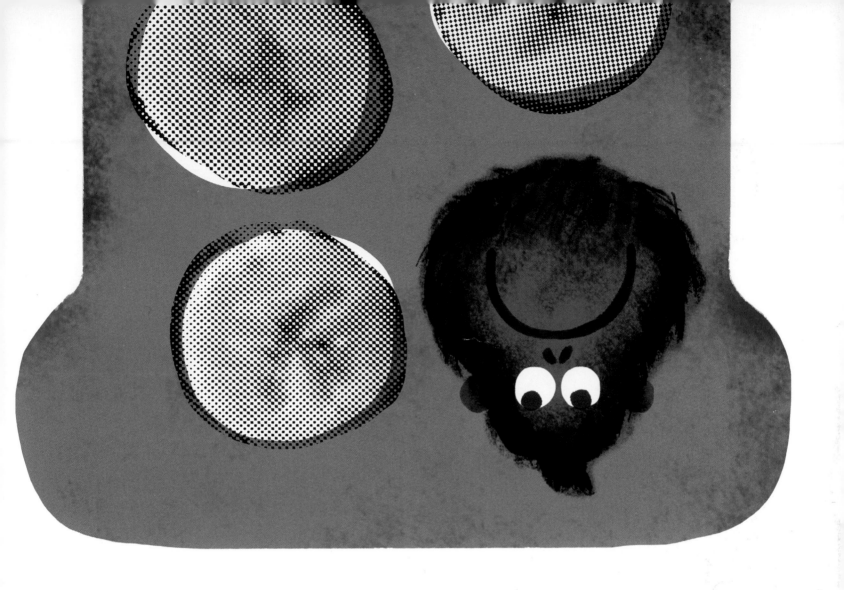

I won't eat one on my head.

I won't eat one up and down,

inside - outside,
right-side, wrong - side,

round the bend,

in the end,
up and under,

I won't

eat a banana.

OK.

You don't have to eat a banana.

HEY!

Where's the banana?

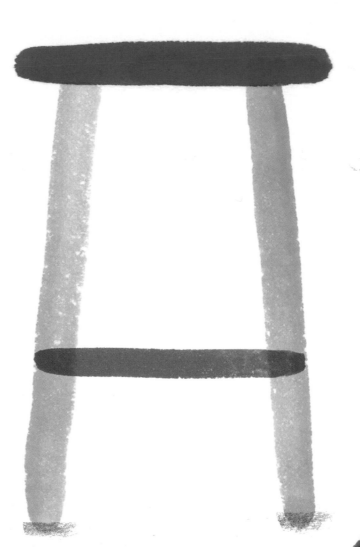

I want another banana.

Say please.

Also by Yasmeen Ismail:

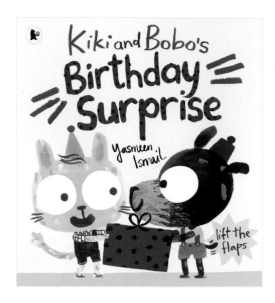

978-1-4063-8006-4

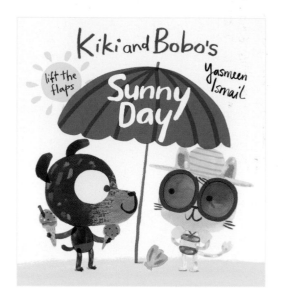

978-1-4063-7887-0

978-1-4063-9096-4

Available from all good booksellers

www.walker.co.uk